The Park Bench Trilogy

Three Sweet Romance Novellas

S.B.ROTH

Contents

The Park Bench Trilogy

Jenny & Sloan

Chapter 1

Jenny sat on the iron bench in the park and looked around. The park was filled with kids and parents. The merry-go-round kept the kids busy, and the ice cream truck filled them with sweet treats. She could see one couple sitting on the grass about twenty feet away drinking what looked like wine, keeping their heads close and the kids away. Clouds in the sky were fluffy and far between while the sun was shining perfectly, it wasn't too hot or too cold.

Smiling to herself she knew today would make someone a great wedding day, but obviously not hers. Her white lace dress that she wore was bought with care, but what did that matter. The groom hadn't shown up. The families stood waiting, but the groom never arrived. She made excuses for him. She couldn't believe she made excuses for him. "Oh, I think he must be stuck in traffic." "When we talked last night, he said he wasn't feeling well." Then one by one everybody left. That's how she ended up on this bench in the park.

Harold, her supposed to be groom, got cold feet. He should have had the decency to at least call it off. Is that what salesmen do? Do they just not show up? Well, that's what Harold Grime did, and Jenny was one angry jilted bride.

Grabbing her cell phone, she spent a few minutes googling the guy she was supposed to marry and lo and behold he had a track record of not showing up for his bride. Apparently, he had not gone to the altar for two other women. Her anger began to rage at this man and then she stopped. The least she could do was blame herself some also. She didn't read this into his profile, but he was far from being committed. She must be partly to blame at least for not checking into this guy she had known for a while.

One after another her tears began to fall, and she took the lace veil laying in her lap and used it as a tissue. After she had given in to the crying urge, she stood up, then sat back down. She didn't know what to do next, so she just sat back and enjoyed the park.

***

On the other side of the park, Sloan was beginning to get worried. He thought Anita, whatever her name was maybe Smith or was it Smythe, would have been here by now. The party had been in full swing for a good forty-five minutes, but still no Anita.

"Sloan," Mr. Andes, his new boss, from the law offices of Andes, Andes, and David, pecked him on the shoulder. "Where is this girl that you're marrying today? I thought she'd be here by now."

"I'm sorry, Mr. Andes, John, ah . . . I called and she must be on her way. I got no answer. I'll call her again and get back with you." Now what was Sloan going to do. Walking toward the merry-go-round he saw a young girl sitting on a bench. Thinking to himself, she's wearing white. She'll do. He had hired a fake preacher now he needed a fake bride.

"I hope this works," he said to himself. Running across the park he grabbed Jenny by the hand and said, "Come with me and I'll explain on the way."

Jenny pulled back, "I'll scream police if you don't stop pulling on me. What do you want?"

"I need a bride to impress my new boss. It's not for real, just go along with it, okay."

Jenny looked at this man, and in a split second asked, "What's in it for me?"

Sloan didn't have time to think. This wedding needed to take place ASAP. "Whatever you want. Let's shake and get going. By the way, your name is Anita right now."

"Whatever I want . . . this is going to be costly. I'm up for this, let's go." Jenny began running with Sloan. The people in the park watched these two run to what appeared to be their wedding venue.

Sloan stopped the musicians from playing and began, "Well, we're a little late, but I found my bride and we're ready to share with all of you our love for this day and forever."

All the guests began to applaud as Sloan and Jenny stood before the preacher and were married in an impulsive ceremony.

"You may kiss the bride." The preacher didn't leave anything out, Jenny thought.

Sloan looked into Jenny's amber eyes and places a solid kiss on her cheek.

"I think we'll save the good stuff for later when we get home." He laughed.

"Where are you going on your honeymoon?" Someone in the crowd yelled.

"Wherever she wants." Sloan yelled back.

Mr. Andes came over and shook their hands. "Where do you want him to take you, Anita."

At first, she didn't answer, the name threw her off. "Oh, I think a European tour would be wonderful." She remembered he said she could have anything she wanted.

"Not sure I can give him that much time off just yet. Maybe something a little shorter would be best." Mr. Andes laughed and Sloan and Jenny (aka. Anita) joined him.

Jenny could not believe what was happening. How did she let herself get caught up in this? Why did Sloan have to get married? Was it a part of the job? Jenny was totally confused and couldn't wait until they were alone, and she could talk freely.

"Sloan," John Andes called to him from across the table. "Why don't you and Anita sit here, and we can get to know her better."

Sloan looked at Jenny and shrugged his shoulders. "Give us a minute and we'll come over."

Jenny just looked at him, "Now what are we going to do? Why did you have to get married so quickly?"

"Well, the law firm only hires married men and when I was interviewed, I told him that I was getting married today . . . in the park. He hired me on the spot and arranged this little party for me to meet everyone. I shouldn't have lied, but I really wanted this job and now here I am trying to explain to you. I'm sorry."

"It's not your fault that I said okay to this crazy scheme. My fiancé just jilted me at the altar. I don't even know why he didn't show. Now I'm in this mess with you and there are so many questions to answer. Now hug me like a loving husband and we'll go sit down and converse for a little while. I'm going to ask him to call me Jenny. I can say it's my middle name and my mother always called me Jenny. How did we meet?"

As they walked toward the table Sloan leaned over and said, "Dating app – Christian Dating."

Sitting down at the table with John Andes, Seth David, and Carol Andes the three people in the Andes, Andes, and David law firm sent Jenny's heart racing. How she got herself in all these crazy positions she didn't know, but here she was again.

"Thank you for coming today. Sloan and I weren't sure if there would be anyone but the preacher and us. We haven't known each other that long, only about six . . ." Jenny trailed off as Sloan picked up the tail end of her conversation.

"Years. We just got back together and decided to marry about two months ago. We knew each other in school, back in Massachusetts." Sloan was nervous. Jenny didn't know any of the backstory and he knew she was flailing around with the conversation.

John just smiled. "Well however the two of you got together, it definitely looks like love. You are perfect for each other. "So have you decided on a honeymoon?"

Sloan wasn't sure what to say, but he spoke right up anyway. "We will wait a little while until I've been at the firm awhile and at least gotten my feet wet."

Seth David, an older gentleman spoke up, "No, no, no. If you get started, you'll never get away. I'll tell you what. I have a condo in Great Shores, Alabama that is right on the water. Pack your things and head out tonight. I'll even spring for the flight and a rental car. Enjoy yourself for the next two weeks. When you get back, be prepared to work and then work some more. How does that sound Anita?"

"Please call me Jenny. My mother loved the name Anita, but I'm not fond of it so I go by my middle name. It sounds lovely, but

I'll need to see if I can take the time off from work."

"What do you do?" Carol Andes asked.

"Well, I'm a social worker at Love is Home Orphanage." Jenny knew she could get the time off, but . . . oh, dear. What now?

Chapter 2

As Jenny and Sloan walked away from the party, they nervously began to laugh. Sitting on the park bench where Sloan had found her, Jenny began to talk.

"Listen, you can tell your boss that we decided to annul this marriage. Anything you want, and I will go away without a word, BUT you promised me whatever I wanted was a go! So, I want those two weeks in Great Shores. Can we do it?"

Sloan thought that was reasonable. "I don't know why not. I'll get tickets from Mr. David; you can go home, and pack then you'll be off for two weeks at the beach. Take whoever you want. I'll stay in my apartment hidden out until this is all over."

"Nope, not going to happen. We are both going. I'll take the bedroom, you can sleep on the couch, and we can take plenty of pictures to show them how much fun we're having. What time are we leaving tomorrow?" Jenny was not giving up this gig for anything. This guy laughed when she laughed and did things on the spur of the moment. Who knew, he might be a lot of fun. She'd call in at work and tell them the circumstances, then she and Sloan would head off in the skies over Kansas to Alabama.

"I think he said the flight leaves at . . ."

"Stop, that's Harold over by that tree that looks like it's dying. Not Harold but the tree. What's he doing?"

"Who is Harold?"

"He's my once upon a time fiancé!"

"Jenny, Jenny," Harold began walking their way and waving. "Jenny, I'm so sorry. I just couldn't. For some reason I couldn't go through with it. Can you ever forgive me?"

Sloan stood and faced Harold, "No she can't forgive you. Now leave. We have plans to arrange." (Sloan winked at Jenny)

Jenny tried to make Sloan sit down, but he refused. "Sloan I'll handle this. Harold, it really doesn't matter what you think or thought." Wondering how she could explain Sloan, she began, "I saw an old boyfriend from school, that's Sloan." Putting her hand on his shoulder. "We were in love back then, and I guess we still are, because we just got married. So, forget you knew me." (Jenny smiled slyly at Sloan)

Harold looked indignant and Sloan looked positively radiant.

"That's right Harold olé buddy!" Sloan almost pulled it off until six foot five, Harold Grime, grabbed his shirt in his fist.

"If you ever hurt this woman, I'll come after you. Remember that!" Harold said his piece then turned and left.

Jenny and Sloan sat down and sighed a big sigh of relief.

"I'm worn out from all the drama!" Jenny had had enough. "Glad Harold believed all that garbage. If I'd known him longer, he might have realized it wasn't true."

Sloan didn't say anything, then began to laugh his head off. When he finally had himself under control he turned to Jenny and smiled. "When I woke up this morning, I thought the craziest thing about today was I was marrying a girl I had never met so I could get a job. Little did I know that it would be crazier than that and now I've married a long-lost love from Massachusetts!" He began to laugh again, and tears rolled down his cheeks.

Jenny couldn't believe he was taking everything so well. Soon she was laughing and everyone who walked by laughed with them.

"Well, if we've gotten that out of our system, there is one more little thing." Jenny was waiting to share this info.

"What is that? It couldn't be any worse than what has happened."

Jenny slowly began, "When Harold and I decided to get married, I told my landlord I would be moving out tomorrow. I need to go pack my stuff and move. Can I put it into your house until we return?" He probably won't laugh now, Jenny thought.

"I do have an empty garage if that will hold it all. Do you need help?" Sloan wasn't sure how much she was talking about, but it couldn't be a lot.

"Only my clothes, and the contents of the refrigerator. The rest belongs to the landlord. It won't take me two hours to get it ready." Stopping to write down her address she handed it to him. "Could you pick me and my junk up at about seven this evening? I can stay at a hotel afterwards if you'd prefer."

"I'll be there, and you'll stay with me. Heck, we're leaving tomorrow so it's no problem."

After sending their phone numbers to each other they parted ways.

Jenny grabbed a cab and headed to her small apartment a few blocks from the park, while Sloan went to the parking lot and drove off in his BMW, headed home to the upper west side of town. Neither hoped they were making a mistake.

Chapter 3

Jenny opened the door to her apartment on the third-floor walk-up and looked around. Dull gray walls, one window and a bedroom about the size of a child's bunk bed. The bathroom was so small that one person had to turn in circles to go from one facility to another. Jenny plopped down in the only comfortable chair in the room. Lord, help me. She wasn't sure if she'd made any right decisions in the last several years. Finishing college was a first in her family, and her job with the orphanage was one she enjoyed completely, but everything after that was a quick slide downward.

Dating had turned into a circus when she joined a couple of dating apps and those quickly went off the rails. She thought she'd found the one when she went out with Harold Grime, yes, she knew he was forgetful, yes, he was ten feet taller than she was, and yes, he called his mother daily, at the same time. (giggling to herself) Jenny realized she had missed, no ignored the warning signs. Then where had this Sloan come from . . . she hadn't even asked his last name. Was she so desperate that she would marry anyone? Well, maybe.

Getting up from the chair, the refrigerator beckoned her. Opening the door, she found some out of date milk, a stick of butter, and two eggs. The freezer held ice cubes. Easier to throw it all away than to carry two eggs and butter to his house.

When she opened the door to her closet it was almost as bad. She wore jeans to work each day so she could get up and down easily with the children. A variety of t-shirts and several blouses plus one nice dress. Oh, and her wedding dress! Packing everything into two suitcases including her bathroom, she was ready to go by six o'clock. Once again, she sat down and in no time, she was fast asleep. The day had worked overtime on her nerves and the only way she could release it was in sleep.

Dreams brought her back to the park where she was standing before an altar of a church looking for her groom. The crowd who had gathered were looking at her with a rather sad look. As she began to cry, her groom began to walk down the aisle, but something was wrong . . . it wasn't Harold Grime . . . it was Sloan, no last name, walking toward her, and she began to smile. The crowd clapped and the preacher was jumping for joy. Then she heard someone banging on the door to the church yelling, "Are you in there, Jenny?" Quickly waking up, Jenny realized it was Sloan at the door.

"How long have you been knocking? I fell asleep in the chair and didn't hear you." Jenny was stretching and yawning.

"Not long, about twenty minutes!" Laughing as he spoke. "I almost had a heart attack walking up the stairs. You didn't tell me you lived in a walkup!"

Jenny loved the way he was always laughing. "I've only got two suitcases."

Sloan looked around at the shabby apartment, he really needed to know more about this young lady. He hoped she was who she appeared to be.

Heading down the stairs, they stopped at the apartment on the bottom floor, and Jenny left the key with the building manager. "Thank you for everything," she said.

"Where did you find a place to park, Sloan?" Jenny knew how hard it was to find parking places on these streets. All she saw was a few BMW's and some really old Chevy's.

"Right in front! Here I am." Opening the door to his pearl white BMW, he grabbed her luggage and stowed them in the back while she sat down on the smooth leather seats.

Rubbing her hands gently on the leather, Jenny began to realize she might be out of her league. She surmised he was a lawyer, but a first-year lawyer wouldn't have this kind of money. Maybe she needed to ask some questions.

Sloan drove slowly as they headed uptown to his home. Jenny talked at length about the comfort of the car, the area they were heading into and the fact that she had grown up in an orphanage until she was adopted at the age of twelve.

Sloan told her that he was an only child to older parents who had lived in Maine where he grew up and had given him way too much. His parents had passed several years ago, although not at the same time.

About twenty minutes later they pulled into the driveway of a nice two-story brick home with manicured lawns and shrubbery. "So, this is where you live," she said.

"Yes, I bought this house right after college with my graduation money. It didn't pay for the entire house, but the money left to me by my parents finished it off. It's just the right size for me and my future family." Sloan was getting a little sentimental, so he got quiet.

"This is just what I've always dreamed of living in with my family. My adoptive parents were poor, so I grew up in a three-bedroom frame that was losing its porch. I have five other adopted brothers and sisters and we all slept in the same room during the winter and in the summer the boys slept on the back porch. My parents weren't always nice to us, but when you realize where you came from, it was better than nothing." Jenny opened the car door and got out, ready to see this home.

"Wow, we could be really depressing people if we aren't careful!" Sloan began to laugh.

"Watch out." Jenny joined him in a good laugh.

Walking into the house Jenny thought, he may drive fancy, but he doesn't live that way. The house was a normal everyday house. Big, yes, but comfortable overstuffed furniture with warm colors and an inviting personality. If a home could have a personality. Bright colors filled in as vases and flowers, anything to give the place a little class.

"Well, what do you think?" Sloan asked as they entered the living area.

"It's very nice. I would have imagined it was going to be a bachelor pad, but it's a comfortable home."

"I told you I wanted it to be just what a family would need, and that's what I told the decorator. She thought I was crazy but here we are!" Sloan loved his place.

Seeing a large wooden H sitting on the fireplace hearth. "What does the H stand for, Sloan?"

"My last name, Harris."

"That was a silly question, wasn't it? But I forgot or wasn't listening when the preacher said Harris when we were getting married. Gosh, that even sounds strange. Glad it wasn't legal. How will you handle that with your boss?"

"Don't worry, it won't be a problem. I think you said your last name was Hart. Is that right?"

"Yes, Jenny Marie Hart. When my adopted parents added a middle name and my last name, I was so proud. No one at my school understood how important that was to me. I had been given the last name Smith at the orphanage, but this last name came with my very own family.

"Let me show you where you can put your bags and then we can go to my favorite restaurant for dinner. Does that sound good?"

"Depends on the food. What's your favorite restaurant?"

"Jimmy's Burgers and Fries – Let us get you loaded! I love the place."

"Wow, I could do with a great hamburger. I'll be ready, show me where to go." Jenny loved burgers and fries with a great strawberry shake. She was shown to a bedroom upstairs that had its own bathroom. "This is perfect. Give me five minutes."

Sloan went back downstairs and called his boss. The conversation centered around airline tickets and condo keys. Mr. Andes told him the tickets were at the counter and the keys would be handed to him when they checked in at the condo. Within those five minutes Jenny was downstairs, freshened up and ready to eat.

Jimmy's was just what she needed. Wooden booths, chrome tables and chairs, it looked more from the 50's than anything else. The music was 50's vintage and Jenny found herself humming some of the old songs. Jimmy himself came over to talk with Sloan and Jenny. Sloan introduced her as his new wife!

"Where's that beautiful ring you should have given your new wife?" Jimmy was eyeing Sloan with a grin.

"It's at the jeweler. Too big, had to be resized." Sloan wasn't sure what to say. He hadn't thought about a ring.

Jimmy wished them well, then went back to the kitchen.

Sloan and Jenny continued eating, but the conversation had lulled, and their minds turned to the trip they were to make in the morning.

Chapter 4

The next day they took their seats in first class and prepared for the journey to Great Shores for their two-week non-honeymoon. Sloan was nervous. He knew very little about Jenny and if he thought long enough, he realized she knew little about him. They had exchanged names and where they grew up, but did Jenny like her steak rare or well-done, or what kind of movies were her favorite? The little things that make for a great friendship. Was that what he wanted was a great friendship or was he already thinking something more?

Jenny bumped his arm, "I'm sorry, even in first class I guess bumping arms is inevitable!" Laughing.

He liked the way she laughed. It started out in her chest and rose quickly before she finally grabbed her tummy then laughing out loud. Jenny laughed a lot, that was one thing he wanted in a wife, the ability to laugh easily. "Are you excited," he asked her.

"You know I've never flown first class before. In fact, I've only flown one other time and it was nothing like this. Have you flown a lot?" Jenny felt uncomfortable and her mouth just kept running. She knew the flight would only be a couple of hours, so she had brought a book. Picking it up she opened and stared at it, rereading the same page over and over.

Sloan took the hint and stayed quiet. Jenny was pretty. Looking at her out of the corner of his eyes, he could see tiny freckles scattered over her nose and forehead. He liked freckles. Once she had gone upstairs to bed last night, he never heard a peep from her, so he assumed she didn't snore. Laughing to himself he noticed Jenny looking over as he laughed, and she smiled. She had a nice smile.

"What are you laughing at now?" Jenny asked.

"I was just thinking that you had a nice smile." Sloan didn't want to bring up snoring.

"So, you're laughing at my smile?" Jenny frowned.

Sloan laughed again, "NO, no I was laughing at something else, but I didn't want to insult you."

"Too late. Why were you laughing?"

"I thought you didn't snore because I never heard a peep out of you last night." Sloan was mad at himself for even thinking it.

Laughing at him, "Well no worries because you snore enough for both of us!"

"What? I don't snore. Do I?"

"I only tell the truth." Grinning at him mischievously. Crossing her fingers out of sight.

The rest of the flight was uneventful. Jenny fell asleep reading her book and her head slowly landed on Sloan's shoulder. Comfy shoulders she thought as she drifted off.

Sloan gently tapped her arm when they were getting ready to land. "We're about to land. Time to wake up and smell the roses!"

"Huh, what roses?" Jenny was a little groggy from her nap. "Didn't take long to get here. I wonder how long the drive is to the condo?"

"I think John said about twenty minutes. The car should be ready when we check in at the counter. Wonder what he rented for us? Sloan thought to himself, probably a family van or something equally ugly!

Walking up to the rental car counter, Sloan gave the lady his driver's license to check in. He watched as she looked up his name then raising her eyebrows just enough, she let him know she was impressed.

"I believe your car is waiting curbside for you. If you'll please go over these papers and sign by the yellow x, you will be good to go." Handing him the papers she continued, "I see you ordered a white Porsche convertible for your ride the next two weeks." As he signed the papers she continued, "Looks like the credit card on file will cover all of your expenses."

Sloan smiled, "Thank you for your quick service."

Jenny was dumbstruck. From a park bench to a Porsche convertible free for two weeks. What kind of firm was this where Sloan would work?

"Can you believe this, Jenny?" Sloan was blown away.

"No, but I can't wait to slide into the passenger seat and take off."

"I thought you'd want to drive to the condo." Sloan grinned and they both laughed.

Jenny continued with, "Only if I can pull the keys away from you."

Walking out the terminal door, a man came right up and handed Sloan keys to their car. It wasn't five minutes before they were riding along the coast with the top down and singing old tunes from the 1950s.

Neither could sing but they had no problem singing Don't Be Cruel by Elvis or Rock Around the Clock by Bill Haley and the Comets. When they finished those, they laughed until they found an old 50s station on SXM and away they went.

They were singing All I Have to Do Is Dream by the Everly Brothers when they pulled up at the condo complex. Turning the radio down, Sloan jumped out of the car saying, "I'll be right back sweet cheeks, don't leave!"

Jenny looked at him and yelled, "Call me that again and I'll be gone before you can say cracker jack!"

Sloan came out of the office quickly, "We have our own garage space, and the condo is apart from this building and directly on the beach. I can't believe this. This is going to be fun. Let's get going Jenny Marie . . . is that better?

"Not much, how about just Jenny." She hated nicknames. They never served her well. At the orphanage she was called names and put down so many times that she just grew to dislike all nicknames. She knew she needed to explain herself, but she'd wait until that evening.

"Looks like we're here already," Sloan pulled into the driveway of a sand-colored stucco home, just the color of the sand around it. The walls facing the Gulf were all windows, which had an excellent view.

Jenny looked around, the water was a beautiful blue and the beach was free of any guests other than from the two condos. The one they were in and the one next to it. "Let's get this party started," she said. Grabbing her bags, Jenny made it to the front door before Sloan. "Hurry, I can't wait to see the inside."

"Hold your horses, just Jen . . . Sorry it's a habit, I'll stop." Putting the key in the lock the door opened easily and he allowed her access first.

The living area was huge with a fireplace and beautiful turquoise and cream furniture that was facing the ocean. "Wow, Sloan. I had no idea it could be this beautiful."

They put bags down and then toured the home. Two bedrooms, so Sloan didn't have to sleep on the sofa. There were two bathrooms so no sharing and then the kitchen. Not only was it filled with new appliances, but the cabinets were also filled with every kind of staple imaginable. When Sloan opened the refrigerator, they found it was full of fresh food, veggies, fruit, and steaks!

Looking at Sloan, Jenny smiled then ran and hugged him. "This is wonderful. Thank you for making me your pretend bride. We're going to have a wonderful two weeks."

Chapter 5

Jenny woke early, put on her jogging shorts, and went for a run on the beach. Breathe she thought. Just breathe! It had been a rough week, but an amazing one. Planning for a wedding, then being stood up, only to pretend to marry someone she did not know. Now she was on this pretend honeymoon in the most fabulous place.

"Breathe, breathe, slowly breathe in, then exhale." She continued this mantra as she ran. Stopping to sit on the beach and watch the waves roll into shore. Beautiful, she thought.

"You took off without me," Sloan said as he sat down beside her. "This place is wonderful. Our own place to run without a thousand sightseers, the waves crashing on the beach. I think I could sit out here forever."

Jenny nodded her head in agreement. "If I'd known you were a runner, I'd have been a little louder this morning and woke you up when I got up."

"I'm really not much of one. Usually, I just walk and enjoy what God has blessed us with in nature. That's why I like the beach. Can you imagine watching Genesis 1:20-21 actually happening? It must have been glorious."

Jenny smiled. She had thought that same thought many times over the years. She had no clue that Sloan was so in tune to God's blessings. "I agree," she said.

Sitting on the sandy beach the two talked about how they might have reacted had that been possible. Sloan began, "I bet I'd have told God the way I might have added to it. I'm always wanting to be the one in charge. Not sure God would have thought my input would be helpful!" Laughing he looked at Jenny. "What about you?"

Jenny thought a minute, "I would have hidden. I'm not sure why, but I'd have hidden the minute God began to do anything Godly! It's the same reason I won't volunteer at church. I'm not sure, I would be good enough." Standing and brushing the sand off her body, Jenny continued, "I'm starving. I'll race you to the condo. The last one who arrives fixes breakfast!" Taking off she realized Sloan was already running and she needed to get on the ball. "No fair," she yelled.

Sloan never looked back. He wasn't going to be last as he huffed and puffed his way down the beach. He thought she could cook way better than he could, so he better be first. That was his last thought before she passed him, and he could tell she would win by several lengths. When had he slowed down, or she had sped up? Losing and being slow just wasn't fair!

Jenny was standing on the back deck trying to catch her breath. "Wow, that took you long enough!"

"Don't gloat, I give up, you won fair and square." Sloan headed inside to start breakfast. "What would you like?"

"Orange juice, fresh squeezed, one egg scrambled, and one piece of wheat toast, please." Smiling at Sloan, Jenny gave him a hug. "I tried to make it easy on you. I'm going to shower. I'll be back before it's ready."

"I've never seen a girl shower in ten minutes." Sloan said to her as she walked out of the kitchen and into her room. Well, maybe she would surprise him, he thought.

Squeezing orange juice was easy, John Andes had a juicer, so that didn't take long, the eggs, and toast was a three-minute cook, and lo and behold when he put it all out on the counter, Jenny walked out of the bedroom.

"Thanks, Sloan. Right on time. Can't wait to dig in, what are you eating? Oh, this orange juice is wonderful."

"I'm eating cereal. Raisin Bran to be exact. I like my cooked breakfast at night." Sloan loved going to the Pancake House in the evenings and having breakfast. It just seemed the right time of the day.

Jenny smiled. "I love a good breakfast at night from the little restaurant around the corner from me. It's called Egg and I; they make a mean steak and eggs too."

Sitting comfortably together at the bar, they finished their breakfast together. Sloan couldn't believe how alike they were. For not knowing each other, they sure got along.

Jenny marveled at the ocean outside the kitchen window. She had put on her bathing suit and coverup before coming in for breakfast. Now she was ready to grab her book and go lounge on the deck. "I'm going to sit outside with my book and read for a while. Is there anything you have planned for today?"

"Not yet. I'll join you after a while. I need to check in with the office, although John will tell me not to worry."

"Well, I'm up for whatever you decide. I'll put the dishes in the dishwasher when I come back inside." Jenny walked to the windows which opened on to the deck and opened them across the back. The best cool breeze entered, and she wanted to enjoy it while she could. It would get hot and humid later. Sitting in her chair she began reading her romance novel.

Sloan picked up his phone and called the office. "Hey, Lucy. Is John Andes in his office?"

"Sure, I'll put you right through, Sloan."

Lucy was very good at her job. Of course, she only had known Sloan for a week before he got married. "He'll take your call, but be ready, he's upset you're calling and not on honeymoon."

Sloan didn't expect him to be upset because he was checking in, "Hello, Mr. Andes. Was just calling . . ."

"Well, you shouldn't be. You're on your honeymoon, sleep in, take your cute wife out to some restaurant."

"She's reading on the deck, and I wanted to tell you how much we love the place. We've taken a run; I fixed her breakfast and we're enjoying our gift. Won't bother you again."

"Enjoy yourselves, Sloan. You deserve it."

Breathing a sigh of relief, Sloan picked up his devotion book for men and walked out to the deck to read. Maybe Jenny would read with him, or at least discuss it.

Chapter 6

Jenny could feel her eyes slowly closing. She needed to get up and move, but she reminded herself this was a vacation. Looking over at Sloan she saw he was into whatever he was reading, so laying her book on the end of her lounger she headed to the water.

Sloan watched her leave, but his devotional was talking about circumstances and how to handle the unexpected ones in life, through Christ. He did take the time to watch her walk to the water. She was graceful, he thought. The minute he thought it she tripped and fell.

Standing she began to laugh and then looked back to see if he was looking. Coast was safe, she thought he didn't see her. Taking off her coverup she ran to the water and jumped in, refreshing but not cold she thought. Maybe the pool would have been better. Looking for seashells took up the next thirty minutes. She found some nice ones, but nothing spectacular.

"Hey, Jenny," Sloan had made his way to the beach and was preparing to body surf on the water. "Have you ever body surfed?"

"Not really, the only surfing I've done is when the waves hit, and I was caught up in the waves and couldn't breathe!"

"Let me show you." Grabbing her hand, he pulled her into the next wave and pushed her up high holding her on top of the wave watching it move her toward shore. "What did you think?"

"I think I don't want to do that again." Coughing up water and sneezing. "Don't ever do that again." Jenny began to walk back to the house. Grabbing her book off the deck and closing the door on her bedroom.

"Wow," Sloan was confused. "Wonder what set her off about that?" Realizing he may have gone a little overboard. He knocked twice on her door. "I'm sorry Jenny. I guess I went a little overboard."

Jenny was embarrassed. She was also angry. Sloan didn't listen to her, and she once again went down into the water and was terrified. It was that boy at the orphanage's fault. The orphanage had taken them to the lake for a day of swimming and a picnic. Jenny was eight and so excited. The home hadn't always gone on day trips, and she was going to be a part of it. She had never seen a lake, much less gone on a picnic.

Boarding the bus to Lake Capucho, she sat by her best friend at the home, Karen. They were both eight and had been at the home for a long time. When they arrived at the lake the two employees had set up an area to eat and then the kids went down to the water.

"Jenny," Karen had called. "Come with me, please."

Jenny had been so afraid, but she wanted to follow Karen. "Wait for the teacher." Jenny said to Karen.

"I'll be all right, don't worry. I can swim." Karen slowly walked to the water holding Jenny's hand. "Just put your feet in, it's so cool."

"Don't let go of me, Karen. Please hold me tight." Jenny wasn't sure about this water adventure. As she looked around, she wasn't sure many of the kids had ever been to the lake. Except that boy, Devon, she thought. He was running into the water and splashing every one of them.

"Come on Jenny," Karen said and pulled her in even further.

Devon had started swimming underneath the water and then pulling the feet out from under the kids and they would go slipping under the water. They moved away from him, still holding hands, they walked a little deeper.

It wasn't long until Devon pulled his trick on them, but this time it was reckless, and tragedy happened. Jenny remembered and began to cry. Both went under hard and fast. Karen hit her head on a rock below the surface and Jenny kept turning over in the water until she finally was pulled up by a teacher.

"Jenny, where is Karen?" The teacher kept asking her.

"She was right beside me."

They found Karen about three hours later. She had been

knocked out when she hit the rock and drowned.

Jenny never went under any water again. Then Sloan doesn't listen to her and here she was, angry at him, at herself and at Devon from so many years ago.

Slowly opening the door of her bedroom, Jenny saw Sloan sitting on the deck with his book. Grabbing her purse, she left a note saying she had gone walking and would be back later. Not to worry, she had overreacted she said. As she closed the front door, Sloan turned and saw her leave.

Chapter 7

Now where is she going? Sloan saw Jenny leave the condo. Maybe she needed to cool off. Walking to the front he saw her walking down the boardwalk headed to the stores lining the main road. He knew she needed some time to think so he went back to his devotional.

Everything had happened so fast. That park bench had been a lifesaver when he found her sitting on it. Funny how life sometimes turns around all with a small little move. The devotional he had been reading was one on anxiety. He definitely needed some input in that area. He had wanted this position with the firm for several years. Working his way into a position had been a work of joy, but his life was all work and no play. He'd never thought about a commitment to someone just to something.

Sitting back, he picked up his book and began to read again. Commitment is a promise and requires planning and sacrifice. Laying the book down he thought about that statement. Asking himself questions was always a good way to get to the heart of the matter, and he had plenty. What was God asking him to commit to? His job? His life? No, he thought. God wanted him to commit to his faith in God. Where he worked, or who he married, was a plan for God to work out and he just needed to commit himself to God. Prayer came to his mind, and he began to pray for Jenny, who he had hurt without intention.

***

Jenny walked down the boardwalk until she found a small coffee shop. As she walked inside, she was drawn to the beach vibes and the fact that they served a cold brew coffee she had been anxious to try. Her first thoughts were those of wishing Sloan were here to try it with her.

Gosh he'd gotten under her skin so easily, she thought. Grabbing the cold brews she walked quickly back to the condo and prepared to hand one to Sloan, but she didn't see him. Walking out of the deck she looked down at the water and there he was on his knees, head bowed, looking closely she suddenly realized he was praying. Not wanting to disturb him, she sat on the deck until she saw him rise.

"Sloan," she called to him from the deck. "I brought you a surprise! Come and get it!"

"I'll be right there." He was so glad he had spent that time in prayer. He felt much better about what he wanted to do in his life.

"I found a place that made cold brew. I've never had any and I wanted to try it, so I got you one too!"

"I've had a few cups. It's all right for hot summer days, but I prefer my hot coffee in the winter. But this is definitely needed right now." Sloan wanted to ask her so many questions but thought waiting was the best option.

Jenny's adventure from long ago needed to be explained in light of the disastrous water incident earlier that morning. "Could you sit down a minute? I wanted to tell you one of my many stories of being in the orphanage."

"Sure, lay it out for me. I've got all the time you need." Grabbing her hand, he walked to the two deck chairs and helped her into one.

Jenny told him the story of the lake visit when she was a mere eight years old. Leaving out no detail she finished with, "and that's why I was so upset when I went under, and you didn't listen to me."

Sloan felt so bad. In the four days they had known each other he had learned so much about Jenny. "I'm sorry about that. I tend to think my way is the only way, and I know it's not. I should have listened. In law school that is one trait we all were to focus on, listening. I failed this time around."

"We all do that, Sloan. I should have just told you the problem, instead of going ballistic and walking out. I guess we both need to listen better."

They sat quietly on the deck, holding hands, and wondering where all of this was heading.

Chapter 8

As the second week drew to a close, Jenny wondered what would happen when they got home. This fake marriage couldn't last forever. They had enjoyed this two-week vacation/honeymoon, but both had to get back to the real world. *Did she really want this to end?* she thought.

Sloan was exactly the kind of guy that she had hoped to find on that stupid dating app she went on, but never found. She loved how he was committed to God and spent time with Him daily. She should be more committed like that, maybe with Sloan's guidance that would happen.

Packing up her few belongs; she found the bag they had used to gather seashells. Thinking back to the fun they had was one of the pluses of the trip. Once they had gotten used to each other they found that they were very much alike. Jenny liked that.

Sloan was in the other room packing up his belongings when Jenny walked into the living area and began throwing out the leftovers in the refrigerator and bagging up the trash to take out before they left.

"Hey, what are you doing?" Sloan had come out of the bedroom and saw her cleaning out the refrigerator. "They have a service that will come in and make it in tip-top shape like when we first arrived. No need for us to dirty our hands!" Laughing as he finished.

"I hate to leave our trash for someone else to find. Just let me take the trash out, please."

Sloan walked over and grabbed the trash bag, grabbing her hand at the same time. Setting the bag down, he turned her around and looked into those gorgeous green eyes, "You are one of a kind, Jenny Marie Hart." Pulling her toward him he looked down and gave her a brotherly kiss on her forehead. Looking back in her eyes he thought, oh what the heck, and planted a kiss on those sweet pink lips he'd wanted to touch since the beginning.

Jenny was taken by surprise, but thoroughly enjoying the moment. She reached behind his neck and gave back as good as she got. Realizing this wasn't good, she turned and grabbed the trash and walked outside.

Leaving for the airport they still hadn't discussed the kiss. Maybe on the flight, she thought. Sloan turned in the rental car they had enjoyed, then they both boarded the shuttle to the airport. Little had been said since leaving the condo, sometimes quiet is good.

Arriving back home, Sloan and Jenny headed to his home.

"You know Sloan, I can't live here. We're not married, really. I'll stay just until I find an apartment." Jenny was not happy. She loved this home.

"No problem. I thought we might go to the place this all started three weeks ago, the park! We can have a picnic and laugh about our trip and what comes next." Sloan hoped Jenny would agree.

"That sounds like a plan. I can look for apartments after the picnic, would you like to help?" Jenny didn't want to leave.

"Perfect."

The next morning Sloan called a small café to make a special picnic lunch. They would pick it up on the way back to the park.

Jenny was ready by ten and they left. She had spent time looking through the advertisements in the paper and online for apartments she could afford. She was ready and determined to find one today.

Stopping at the Le Chic café to pick up the lunch, they drove over to the park.

Looking out the car window and pointing, Jenny said, "Sloan, there's the bench where I was sitting when you found me crying my eyes out."

Sloan laughed. "Yes, but it turned to laughter pretty quick! I'm so glad I found you."

Jenny smiled. She was so glad she had found him, too.

Parking the car, they both grabbed for the picnic basket. "I'll carry it, Jenny. May I hold your hand as we walk?"

"Wow, so formal! Of course, you may do whatever you wish!" Jenny laughed.

As they sat down on the bench, Sloan began to review everything that had happened and more.

"You know, Jenny. One thing I learned while we were away is you are a good person to be around. You know when to laugh, when to be quiet and when to ask questions. I'm not sure I've ever met anyone like you before."

"Well, I like that you laugh so easily, your heart is really good, you listen to what God says and appear to be committed to Him. Sloan you care about everything and everyone, I like that."

Sloan stood and got down on his knee. "Jenny, I know I've done this before, but I believe God brought you to me. I know it's quick and I know we don't know a lot about each other. But what I do know is that God brought you to this park to marry me. Now let's do it for real!"

Jenny was stunned. This was what she hoped for, dreamed, and now reality. "Oh, Sloan . . . YES!

The Park Bench Trilogy

Susan & Levi

Chapter 1

Susan came to the park every day, rain, or shine. It was here that she said her prayers and read her devotions, and even in the rain she found it comforting knowing that God was in charge of the weather. He would provide. And He did.

She had been sitting on her bench when she saw a couple arrive and watched as the man proposed and the girl had said yes. How happy they appeared. She watched as they ate their picnic lunch and held hands. She was happy for them; she said a prayer for both of them.

Today her devotion was from the *Daily Nosh*, an online Messianic Jewish Devotional. It was
right on target with her thinking that God would provide. *When Yeshua turned water into wine, He supernaturally produced excellent not poor or mediocre results. When God moves in our lives to meet our needs, we should expect and believe that the result will be of the highest quality and for our greatest good.*
This was the commentary for John 2:10 and Susan knew God would provide her with a husband that He had picked out for her.

Thinking to herself about John 2:10, she wondered where Levi was this morning. He was never late. They always played a game of chess after they had finished their daily Bible reading and discussion. She had met Levi several months ago. Both come to the park, find a bench, and complete their devotionals for the day. She had watched him for several weeks before finally nodding her head in acknowledgement and then introducing herself a week later, he sat near and introduced himself.

She discovered they were both in their twenties and finishing the last year of college. He was working towards a degree in science technology while she was wanting to teach elementary school. They had built a friendship through discussions of Yeshua and the game of chess.

****

Levi was running late. He didn't want to miss seeing Susan at the park, but that is exactly what was going to happen. One of his classes was rescheduled, and he had forgotten so he ran late to class and then had to stay and have a meeting with his professor.

Trying to be on the fast track to graduation, he knew to be aware of his time and his projects. This class had a rather intensive project that he had been working on for months and he needed some help from the professor.

"Thank you for your help today, Professor Franks. That one little piece was really stopping my process to finish."

"No problem, Levi. You had the answer. Just a little push was all you needed." Professor Franks liked Levi and hoped he moved forward towards his master's and then doctorate.

Hurrying from the classroom, Levi ran to the park and watched as Susan stepped up onto the bus that would deliver her back to her apartment. *Dang, I can't believe I'm late*, he thought.

Sitting down on his usual park bench he began to study his devotional reading for the day. He knew that Susan read from the *Daily Nosh*, but he read from numerous devotional books. Levi thought that accepting Jesus was his calling. His parents had raised him in the synagogue. He had completed classes in the Torah, and his parents had celebrated with a bar mitzvah for all his friends. But everything seemed empty. He knew there was something more, so he had started going to a small Christian church and found his savior, Jesus. He hadn't shared with his parents, yet. He just told them he wasn't going to synagogue anymore.

***

Susan had to go to class. She boarded the bus that would take her back to school and as she turned around, she had seen Levi hurrying to the park. *Oh well*, she thought. He was running over an hour late. She was disappointed, but she hoped to see him tomorrow.

She was hurrying to her last education class. Today the class was presenting a project that had been in the works for the semester. Susan's project was centered on bilingual students in a classroom. In theory it would bring those students who felt ostracized in class to become a part of and help the rest of the class embrace them. She had used it with a few of her students in a Sunday School class she attended, and they thought it was great. It was simple but made a big impact. She couldn't wait to share with her instructor.

"Professor Lind, may I present first today?" Susan always wanted to go first. She would compare herself to others if she didn't, but it wasn't going to happen today.

"I'm sorry Susan, but Ginger asked before you arrived. You may go second." Professor Lind enjoyed having Susan in class. She was adventurous in her projects and was always wanting the students to excel. She would hate to lose her once she graduated, but the kids she would teach would be blessed with her as their teacher.

Chapter 2

Levi was at the park thirty minutes early the next morning. He had brought bagels and coffee to share with Susan as they discussed their devotionals. He left the portable chess game back at his place. He had something he wanted to discuss with her, but she didn't come. Now why didn't she come today? He'd never known her to miss a day.

Missed her yesterday, she doesn't come today, I hope all is okay. Levi thought.

"Did you lose your chess partner?" One of the men asked. "She's usually here every day. I think she waits for you." He smiled and raised his eyebrows.

"I think we just missed each other by seconds yesterday." Levi commented. "Do you know her last name? I'd like to find her."

"No, don't really know anyone around here, except Chester. He's the guy I play chess or checkers with when I'm here and he's not here today either."

Levi thought a minute, "She's probably doing something at her school. She is about to graduate."

Sitting back down, Levi was determined to finish his devotion and then head back to his place. He figured he'd see her tomorrow. His devotional reminded him to know his ultimate objective, don't be distracted by lesser objectives and be focused. Pursue God's calling and the assignment he has given you. Even when it is complete you must never stop moving forward or give up.

Levi must concentrate on his graduation and finding a fulfilling position so he could one day find a woman God had chosen for him and have a family. Smiling, Levi prayed that woman was Susan. He could picture her curly black hair and rosy cheeks from sitting in the cool air. Her blue eyes always looked at him with laughter in them. Yes, he wanted to marry her. But first he needed to know her last name, and then laughed at himself. He must be meshuga, he really hadn't known her long enough to be thinking this way.

***

Susan was excited while presenting her project. The professor asked many questions and the other students chimed into the conversation. When it was over, Susan was satisfied that she had done the work that was needed, and her project was exceptional.

Later that afternoon she attended a job fair event at the college. Knowing she would be graduating soon she was looking for the place God was sending her. Walking around there were tables decorated to draw the individual in and capture their attention. As she looked around something nudged her toward a table with a blue cloth covering it. Sitting behind the table was an elderly woman reading a book and relaxing. The woman reminded Susan of a bubbe who was waiting for her grandchild to arrive. Curly grayish hair and a pair of gold wire rimmed glasses helped her to read, and Susan felt drawn to her. As she looked at the information on the table, the woman began to introduce herself.

Although she had difficulty standing, she did and then began to introduce herself. "Hi, I'm Betty. Has God drawn you to join the mission field?"

Susan had not thought about missions, but something had been on her heart for a while, and she needed to know more about this opportunity. "I'm not sure. Tell me more about this *Bible International* program, please."

"Well, . . . let's see, first, what is your name?"

"Susan . . . Susan Katz."

"Well, Susan Katz, this organization has been around for a very long time. We meet people where they are, work with them in their language and most of all tell them about Jesus. Are you just graduating from school?"

"Yes, I will have my elementary education degree. Is there an area for teachers?" Susan was becoming very interested.

"As a fact, there is an area. When my husband and I joined Bible International I too was a teacher, and he was a translator. We were with them our entire married life. Are you married or engaged?"

"No ma'am." Looking at the pamphlets.

Betty began putting the information together. "My number is on the back if you want to call me. Maybe I can come to your house and speak to your parents also."

"I'll call you." Susan knew she was headed for a collision course with her parents, but they were loving and patient. They would be disappointed at first but would come to accept her decision.

***

Levi set up his chess pieces on Thursday morning and waited for Susan to arrive. Just as usual, she appeared and sat down with him to play a morning game of chess.

"Why aren't we doing our devotionals first?" Susan quietly questioned.

Levi allowed the curve of his mouth to move upward until a smile formed. "I have missed our games. After we play, then we will praise our God for giving us this time. I have also missed you and realized I know nothing about you except your first name and that you are in school to be a teacher. Maybe we can share a little more over a game of chess?"

Susan sat back in her chair. Looking over her chess partner, she too realized that they knew little about each other. Jesus and being Jewish was their connection. "I think I'd like that. I'm not sure I will have time for our devotional today. It is the last day of classes and I need to check in this afternoon with all of my professors."

"I need to do that also. I will finally be finished. Now to figure out what to do with my degree."

"Where is God leading you, Levi?"

"I wish I knew. It's hard to not know what he wants from us." Levi had been struggling for the full semester on where to apply.

"All right let's get started on our five-minute date interview! If we don't start now, I'll have to go again. I understand you're wondering where God wants you. Yeshua often makes me be patient."

Levi grinned, "Would you like to go first?"

Susan shook her head no so Levi began.

"I am Levi Garten. I grew up in this community and attended synagogue close by. School was school, no awards, but a pretty good grade point average. One that helped me get into college and earn a degree in languages."

"What languages can you speak, fluently?"

"Fluently, right now, Spanish, English, Hebrew, and Greek, and I can read and write Latin."

"That's amazing. Now tell me about your parents, siblings?"

"No siblings, only child, and my parents are alive and well. My father works in finance, and my mother works in our jewelry store. Both would like for me to work in the store, but it's boring. I worked there throughout high school and college, so I'm over that!"

After a few minutes he said, "Your turn. Leave nothing out!"

"I am Susan Katz. I too am an only child, and my parents are still living. They don't know that I have accepted Jesus, and I attend a small Christian church on the other side of town. They would probably disown me. But I must tell them, and I am graduating with a degree in education."

"That can't be all."

"That's all I'm telling you today," Susan said and began to laugh. "Let's play chess."

Chapter 3

"That was a good game, Susan. Too bad you missed a move. I think you would have won if you had caught it." Levi was trying not to gloat. "Will you be back tomorrow morning?"

"I've got a few errands to run so probably not. School is about to end; I have a job interview of sorts and I really need to talk with my parents. I'll see you next Monday, does that work?" Susan asked with a smile on her face. Getting up when she saw her bus she started to walk away.

"Where is your job interview? Good Luck." She didn't hear him and kept on walking, turning only to wave as she got on the bus.

Waving goodbye, Levi grabbed his bicycle, his only mode of transportation at the moment, and took off towards town. There was a job fair at the community center in his area and he thought he'd check it out. Maybe God would move him toward the perfect job to spread his Word.

Before entering the community center, Levi bowed his head and prayed that God would provide a place for him where God could use him. There were businesses, schools, and other job-oriented people filling the rooms and halls of the community center. Walking up and down the aisles, Levi stopped at many tables to look over the information, but nothing seemed to be the right place. One business was willing to pay off all his school loans and all his expenses for a year, but he wasn't sure.

Sitting at a small lunch table drinking coffee and eating a sandwich would give him some thinking time, he thought.

As he sat down, an elderly lady approached and set down her cup. "May I have a few words with you sir? I'm looking for a particular type of individual to work in an area that few can obtain."

Levi looked confused, "Of course. Have a seat. I'm a little confused as to why you would want to speak with me, but I am looking for work. I will graduate with my degree in languages and want to make sure I find a place that God has led me to work."

Putting out her hand, "Shake my hand Mr. . . . Mr.?"

"Garten, my name is Levi Garten."

"I'm with Bible International and we are looking for Godly people to translate work into the original language of many peoples around the world. My name is Betty, I go to these job fairs to share my experience and hand out materials for others to pray about and maybe one day they will come and share God's message with us."

"Sounds interesting. Where are the offices?" Levi wanted to learn more. He wanted to work with languages and not in an office.

"Our main offices are scattered in many places around the world., I'd like to encourage you to tour one of our language facilities located in the Southwest."

"I'll take this information with me. Do you have a number where I can reach you?" This opportunity really interested Levi. He would discuss with his parents and get back with her.

Levi found three other job possibilities as he toured the job fair. Two seemed quite promising, but he kept coming back to the Bible information. He could use all of his languages and maybe learn a few more. Apparently, they had a language school which would prepare him for placement. He'd like to talk with Susan, but that might not happen for a few days, so his parent conference would be first. After he got through that, he'd have a better understanding (he hoped) of God's plan for him.

***

Susan spent the better part of the afternoon touching base with each professor. Many had heard of Bible International and encouraged her to discuss it with her parents.

"Susan, I know your parents don't know about your conversion, but if you are a solid Christian as you say, then God will smooth your way as you discuss with them." Professor Lind stated as she hugged Susan good-bye.

The bus ride home seemed very short to Susan. She didn't have time to prepare what she would say to her parents. She hated to disappoint them. She prayed the entire time she was on the bus and all she could think of was Jeremiah 29:11. *"For I know the plans I have for you . . ."* Yes, He did.

Opening the door to her home, she was greeted cheerfully by her mother. "I'm so glad you're home. We have so much to discuss. I know you've been to a job fair. What did you discover?"

"Oh, Imma," which is what she had always called her mother. "I have so much to decide and so much to tell you and Daddy. Is he home?"

"Little one, he will be here soon. Let's have a snack." Her mother was always pushing food at her, even when she thought she wasn't hungry.

About an hour later, Susan's dad came in the back door. "Oh, daddy, I'm glad you're home."

"What do you need now, little Susie." Putting his arm around Susan, he hugged her and then they began to dance. This was the nightly ritual whenever they were together.

Susan loved this daddy-daughter dance they did. Some of her friends thought it was corny, but she knew it was special and when she married, she and her father would dance this dance together on her wedding day.

"I think I've found a job. I went to a job fair at the school and talked with a lady who I liked very much. She gave me some information. I want you to look at it and see what you think. I showed Professor Lind and she thought it was a perfect fit for me."

Mr. Katz took the information and laid it aside. "Now let me wash up for dinner. Then I will look it over. We can talk later."

Susan knew the hardest part was yet to come.

Chapter 4

After dinner Mr. Katz walked into his study and shut the door. Susan was worried, but she stayed in her room and prayed as she waited. It wasn't long until there was a knock at her bedroom door.

"Susan," her mother said. "Your father would like to see you in his study."

Susan could tell nothing by her mother's tone. Maybe all will be well. "I'll be right down."

Walking into the study, her Daddy and her Imma were sitting side by side on the small leather loveseat. Susan sat in the matching chair opposite the love seat.

"Well, your mother and I have read the information and we have a few questions. First, did you realize this is a Christian organization?"

"Yes, father I did. You know that I have not been attending temple for a long time, and I have found a home in a small church on the other side of town. I feel that in order to grow I need to see how I fit in to a Christian organization such as this one. I will still be teaching children, but it might be in a country where they don't have teachers, and it won't be one where Christians are persecuted. They need people to share the Word and to share their love."

"Well, said. But you are a Jew. What if you are placed in a school in Palestine or an area of the world which is not favorable to Jews?"

"I promise father that I will make sure that doesn't happen. All I want is your blessing to pursue this calling."

"I am disappointed that you have chosen to leave the Jewish faith, but I want to learn from you the why, and I promise also to be open minded. We want you to be happy. Please do not abandon your Jewish roots."

"I promise Daddy, I promise." Flying into her parents arms she cried and hugged them. Thank God for His intervention.

***

Levi knew it was now or never as he walked into his house. His mother was putting supper on the table and his father was reading the newspaper. He had decided to wait until after they had eaten. He knew his father well enough to know that if he was totally displeased, he would slam the study door and not come out, so it would be better after they had eaten his mother's meal.

"I'm home. Sorry I'm a little late. Went to speak with my professor and I went to a job fair this afternoon also."

No one said much, just nodded their head.

"So, you're not interested in working in the jewelry store with me, Levi?" His mother always through the guilt trip on him.

"I don't think so mom. It would be a waste of my degree. I don't mind helping out if I'm needed, but not full time, okay." Levi stopped talking he didn't need to answer any questions, just yet.

Looking at the table his father sat down, offered the blessing then commented. "Were any of these people at the job fair looking for someone that could speak to them in several different languages?" Smiling when he finished.

Levi knew his father was giving him a hard time. In the world they lived in you met different people from different countries and it was much easier for everyone if you spoke their native language. "Several thought I was highly qualified." Grabbing a slice of roast and potatoes, Levi continued. "What did you do today, Father?"

"Numbers, son, always numbers."

"Does it make you happy to work with numbers all day?" Levi was about to make a point.

"Why, yes it does, Levi."

"Then you understand my need to work with languages. I found one place where I would go to several different areas, teaching them about their language and how to read and write it. Then I could translate it for them into a book or books they could read."

His mother and father felt Levi's excitement.

"Levi, let's finish eating then you and your father can sit down and discuss this decision together."

Things were quiet for the next ten minutes, then father asked, "Dessert. Do we have dessert?"

"Of course, we do. You two go settle in the living room. I'll clean up the table and bring coffee and dessert in a few minutes."

Sitting down in the small but well decorated living area, father and son said nothing until dessert arrived. Levi's mother placed strawberry shortcake in front of them with two cups of coffee. His mother only made this dessert when she knew that he would need some support. Levi laughed to himself. She knew he would be leaving.

"Well, Levi," his father began. "Where have you found a place for your degree?"

"I told you it was a place that would be perfect, but I haven't really told you why it is the right place for me." Stopping for a moment he took a bite of his dessert and then a sip of coffee.

"Get on with it son. Don't worry. I will try to understand. You are a grown man; your decisions are yours alone." He too decided to have a bite or two of his favorite dessert. The coffee helped clear his mouth and prepare him for another bite.

"I am prepared to work for Bible International. I am going to visit a center in either Tucson or Colorado Springs to see how this all works. If it is what God wants for me, then I am prepared to work for them. I knew I needed to talk to you first. I don't want you to be disappointed in me. I am a Jew first, but I love Jesus and must share all He has taught me."

Levi was quiet. He was too emotional to eat another bite of his dessert. He sat on the edge of his chair waiting for his father to answer him. Sitting quietly, he watched his father as tears entered his eyes, fell to his cheeks, and then dried up.

"Levi, you are my only child. I want you to be happy. If this is what you want then go, but please remember you are a chosen one. You are part of God's original family. Teach others about God. I will not stop you." Levi's father was heartbroken, but he understood, a man will do what a man must do.

Levi got on his knees and laid his head on his father's knee. "Thank you, father. I will not disappoint you."

Chapter 5

Susan couldn't wait to see Levi and tell him about her talk with her parents. They weren't overjoyed, but they wouldn't stop her from pursuing her dream. She had called Betty and they were to meet for lunch at Le Chic café near the park to fill out information and to plan on a visit to one of the centers.

Coming to the park was such a ritual for both Susan and Levi, yet in the few weeks or so it seemed they had missed each other at every turn. Susan hoped they met today.

Sitting on her usual park bench she took out the Daily Nosh and began to read the devotional that was written for the day. Susan could always count on the devotional being right on point. Waiting for an hour, she realized that Levi wasn't showing up again, so she sat back and waited for her next meeting time with Betty.

As noon grew close, Susan walked to the cafe and sat down inside at a booth. It wasn't long until Betty arrived, and they began planning.

"Are you excited, Susan?" Betty knew she was, but she loved seeing the excitement in Susan's eyes.

"Yes, ma'am. I tried to meet up with a friend, but they didn't show up. I wanted to share my good news with them."

"Did you call them?"

"I know this sounds strange, but I don't know their number. We never got around to exchanging and now it's too late."

"Young lady, it's never too late. Just let God work in His timing, not yours."

Betty and Susan talked, signed papers, ate, and Betty handed her a ticket to the language center in Colorado Springs.

"You are to be there this Thursday. Wendy Farmer will pick

you up at the airport and take you to the dorms. She'll help get you all settled then you will take a tour of the facility. I'll see you back here the following Monday. Does that sound good for you?"

"Yes, I can't wait."

"It will be chilly, so bring the appropriate clothes."

"I will. I'm so excited."

Susan's parents took her to the airport on Thursday morning, hugged and wished her well, then left. Susan prayed they would understand and come to know Jesus. The flight was uneventful and landed on time. She found Wendy waiting for her and they drove to the language center.

"We're so glad to have you here, Susan. Is this your first time in this area?" Wendy was a little older than Susan, but she was well versed on her job at the school.

"I've never been to Colorado. It's beautiful here." Susan looked at the mountains as they drove to the school.

"I'll take you to your dorm and then come back for you later. We'll do a little touring at that time. You might want to take a short nap if you're tired."

"Thank you, Wendy."

Susan walked into the dorms and was led to a small room on the second floor. Closing the door, she laid down and was fast asleep.

***

Levi walked to the park on Friday, hoping to see Susan, but it didn't happen. His time had been filled with filling applications, meeting with others from Bible International and preparing for his trip to Tucson and the language school.

His hope to see Susan had filled his mind, and he was angry at himself that they hadn't exchanged numbers. He knew she was busy finding a job and he wished her luck, but he really wanted to talk about his discussion with his parents.

He met with Betty on Thursday afternoon, and he was flying out that evening.

Gerald Rose was to meet him at the airport and help him get settled. The drive from the airport was long and the scenery was flat and dusty.

"What do you think of our landscape?" Gerald said with laughter. "Other than the one mountain, it's pretty mundane, don't you think?"

Levi smiled, "It's so different from what I am used to, but I think I like it. Maybe I could work in this area."

"Here's the dorms. Just go inside and they will show you to your room for the weekend. I'll see you later at the group meetings." Gerald drove off and Levi picked up his pack and went inside.

The weekend was fast and furious. Levi knew this was where God was planting him. He couldn't wait to make it official and find out where he fit best. He also couldn't wait to see Susan. Surely, they wouldn't miss each other again.

***

Susan was tired when her plane landed that Monday, going straight to her apartment to unwind. The time in Colorado Springs was well spent and she couldn't wait to tell her parents that this is what she wanted to do no matter where Bible International would send her.

Tuesday morning, she got up and made her way to the park hoping to see Levi before she went to her parents' home. Waiting for over an hour he didn't show, so she left a note with one of the chess players they knew and asked him to be sure and give to Levi. She knew it was a long shot, but it was all she could think to do.

Levi flew in on Wednesday.

Chapter 6

Levi was so excited. Bible International had offered him a job. He would do three months of training at the language school in Tucson and then three months in Colorado Springs prior to being sent to his assigned area.

"You will be a great asset," Mr. Chambers had told him in his final meeting. "Someone with such a command of languages and especially Latin will help our translation division immeasurably."

At twenty-three Levi felt blessed. He knew God had placed him here. Now to tell his parents, and then prepare to move first to Tucson. They housed their own people, so he was excited to find a car and drive out to Arizona. His first stop was the park.

Looking around he saw a few people he knew but no Susan. Why was God keeping them apart? Answering his own question he thought, He is preparing us in some way. God will bring us together soon.

Seeing Chester sitting on what Levi called, 'Susan and Levi's bench', he walked over. "Chester, how are you? Haven't seen you in a while."

Chester smiled. "You've been nonexistent too. What have you been up to, friend?"

"Well, I seem to have found a job and I'll be leaving town and traveling for a while. Has Susan been around lately?"

"Not really. She's come by a few times but doesn't stay long. I think she may have been looking for you. She gave me a letter for you, but I left it in my other jacket. I'll bring it next time, so come back."

"I'll come by tomorrow. Will that work?"

"Sure. Gotta go now, see you!" Chester stood and using his cane, he walked slowly and ambled away.

Levi hoped that Chester didn't forget the note. He needed Susan's phone number. How could he have not gotten it before now?

***

Susan was in a pickle. That's what her mother said to Susan when she needed to buy a car.

"You can't even drive. Do you think your father will buy you a car to drive across country when you're just learning how to drive? You, my daughter, are in a pickle."

"I need transportation when I get to Tucson. If I'm not driving, how will I get around? I have to drive to school, and then back to the dorms. Maybe I could buy a good bicycle when I get there."

"Now that's a good idea. Do you know how far you will be from your classes?" Imma was trying to be sensible with Susan.

"Three miles, maybe, that's too far to walk, but not too far to ride. That's a great idea. I'll purchase a good bicycle." Susan was glad she had solved that problem. Now to get to Tucson in a few days with all her stuff. She was moving and wouldn't be home for at least six months. Excitement filled her soul. She couldn't wait.

"Do you think Dad will drive me to Tucson?" Susan knew the chances were slim to none.

"You can ask, but don't get your hopes up. Maybe we can ship all you will need and then you fly as you did last time. Would that work?"

"I suppose it will have too." Susan continued to pack clothes, leaving some of her cold weather clothes in her closet, but taking items that would work for the Arizona climate. She could buy what she needed when she arrived.

Susan had spoken with her church family about her decision to join Bible International. The congregation had prayed over her and taken a love offering. Several members had committed to helping sponsor her in her spreading of the Word, so she had set up a bank account for the church to deposit the money. She couldn't believe the love that her church was showing to her.

A few days prior to leaving, Susan stopped at the park bench where she and Levi had met. She looked around for Chester, but he wasn't around. She wondered if Chester had seen Levi and given him the note. Thinking to herself she answered, *I guess if he had gotten the note he would have called.*

She hated leaving without speaking to him, but her fire for sharing the Word of God was the most important thing in her life. If Levi was to be, then God would bring them full circle. What a wonderful God she would serve.

***

Levi had made his way to the park every day, but Chester hadn't been there, nor had Susan. Sitting on the bench he had prayed for God to intervene and bring them together again. When he finished Levi realized that he was praying for something he wanted, not what God's will would be for their lives. Once again God reminded him that Levi was not in charge. *Amen,* Levi thought to himself.

Getting in his new to him car that Monday morning, Levi waved to his parents as he pulled out of the driveway. Looking back at the one-story brick home where he had grown up. Tears formed in his eyes. So many good memories. He remembered when his mother had planted the front flower bed, and the puppy which Levi had just gotten, dug up every flower as soon as they were planted. He'd learned a lot about puppies and how to replant a flower bed that day!

Taking to the open road, Levi was ready for his new adventure. This job was a gift from God. Not only could he share about Jesus, but he would be learning so much.

Chapter 7

Susan had shipped all her needs to Arizona. Her flight was scheduled for Tuesday morning and of course, she was excited. Walking around the apartment she grew up in was bittersweet. Her room looked a little forlorn with all her trinkets and bobbles put away. Her mother had commented on how different it looked. She had spent a lot of time on her knees in this room.

As she walked into the kitchen, she found her mother baking cookies. Susan knew that those cookies would make it through all the TSA checks as long as she shared a cookie or two.

"Are those all for me to take?" Susan knew some would stay at home for her father, but she had to ask anyway. It was what they did.

"You always ask that question, and you know the answer." Her mother laughed.

Going down the two flights of stairs, Susan sat on the stoop and looked at all the buildings surrounding her home. She could remember learning to walk on these sidewalks, and the lady down the street, Mrs. Sharber, who always had lemonade for her to drink, or Mr. Klatch, who came and walked with her just to make sure she didn't fall down. As tears of remembrance ran down her cheeks her father walked up and put his arm around her.

"All will be well, little one. Our God, who provides for His people will cover you in all ways. Come in for some cookies and milk." Mr. Katz rose and took Susan's hand. Helping her up he thought how grown up she was, he would miss her.

Tuesday entered like a storm. Susan hadn't slept a wink that night, and her parents were up bright and early to see her off.

"Oh, momma, I'm not going to make it without you and dad. Please pray for me. I love you." Hugging her parents as the share ride had pulled up. "Please don't forget me!"

Her parents smiled, "How can we forget such a troublesome, but lovely young lady. You are our heart and soul. Write and call. We will too."

Getting in the car the driver introduced himself, and she waved goodbye to her parents. Setting out on a new adventure.

***

The training session for Bible International was three months long. Levi would be in classes in the morning, then he would travel to nearby villages to minister to the needs of those areas. The areas were very poor, and they were always excited to see people from the school coming to visit.

Monday was the first day of classes. His first class was called Bible 101. Sounded kind of boring to Levi, but he knew you could never learn enough about the Word. He had his small but sufficient dorm room set up perfectly. It was one bedroom, a small efficiency kitchen then a living area with a table, a couch and one chair. They even provided a small television, although he wasn't sure when he would watch it.

When he arrived, Gerald Rose had been in the office, and he found his first friend. Gerald was also a Messianic Jew and loved working for Bible International. As days before classes began, Levi found himself talking with others that explained all that he had questioned about the job. He learned that everyone worked at their own speed, and that ministering and teaching about Jesus was of utmost importance.

Sometimes at night he prayed that Susan would find a fulfilling job as he had. She was perfect for teaching little children about the glory of Jesus. Maybe when he went home to visit, he could try to find her again. He so enjoyed their friendship.

***

Susan loved her small dorm room. She had put all the trinkets and baubles from her bedroom into her new apartment and it looked just like home. She was already homesick. Mostly she missed talking with Levi, in fact she thought she had seen him crossing the campus on Saturday, but when she got closer it was someone else.

She was ready for classes. Her first class was Ministering with the Word. She couldn't wait to see what God had planned for her. Meeting several new students in her class she and the others went to lunch that week prior to their daily treks into the mountain areas to witness. Tucson was huge, but there were so many hurting people to see. All of this was part of understanding and preparing oneself for where they were to be sent.

Susan especially liked a girl about her age, Joanna. She had a degree in languages like Levi and she began to understand a little more how everything fit together into one ministering packet.

On Friday they would meet with all the other classes and pair up to go out on their own. Susan was a little nervous, but excited at the same time. She hoped to pair up with Joanna or Kathryn, another girl she had met. Kathryn had been on assignment for a year in Poland and was back for some relaxation and refreshing.

"You're going to love wherever you are sent!" Kathryn was about eight years older than Susan and full of information. "I was so afraid when they sent me alone to Poland to teach an English college class! I had forgotten God would actually be doing all the work." Laughing to herself. "It was wonderful. I hope to go back after my next placement. Then I can do six months in the states and six months in Poland."

"My goodness," Susan exclaimed. "How exciting. Where do you think you will go this time?"

"If I'm lucky it will be to a reservation in the states. I so want to make sure all their stories are told in their own language. That is difficult, but I can do it."

"I'll see you in the morning, Kathryn. What time does the bus leave again?"

"I believe we take off at nine tomorrow. Don't be late or you won't get a good seat!"

Chapter 8

Two buses were waiting in front of the school when Levi arrived. One bus was going to one of the reservations near Tucson, and the other was going to homeless shelters in and around Tucson. He hadn't been assigned to one or the other, but he thought he would prefer the reservation bus. Deciding to wait until some friends came along before he made a choice. He waited.

Gerald arrived about five minutes later. He and Levi boarded the reservation bus while most of the other individuals arriving were boarding the homeless shelter bus. Levi kept up a steady conversation with the people around him and those who had already been sharing what to expect.

Not sure he had made the right choice; Levi knew that next time he would go to the homeless shelters. In order to spread God's message, he needed to be comfortable wherever he landed!

As he looked out, he saw the instructors talking and, in a few minutes, they boarded each bus. "We seem to have an overload on the bus going to the shelters, therefore, some of them are coming to this bus. Please move in and allow others to sit down. Now how many empty seats do we have."

Levi spoke up, "I count five."

"Thanks, Levi. Everyone get comfortable and in a minute three to five individuals will join us then we can leave."

The other instructor spoke up, "It will take thirty minutes to arrive at the reservation area."

Levi picked up the book he had brought along and began reading. The story was compelling, and his attention was totally immersed in the story. As he turned a page, he saw two feet standing in front of him, looking upward he saw Susan Katz, staring at him.

"Oh my gosh, what . . .," jumping up he hugged her and hugged her some more. "How did you get here? Have you been here all the time? I couldn't find you at the park. I knew God would work this out."

Quietly Susan tried to calm him down. "Slow down Levi. I'm as shocked as you are. I looked for you everywhere and even left a note with Chester when I couldn't contact you. I had no idea that you were talking to Bible International also. When did you get here? Why haven't we seen each other before today?"

The entire bus of people were staring and wondering who this girl could be, Levi had never said anything about a girlfriend. Listening to their conversation everyone figured out what had happened about the same time the bus driver told everyone to sit down.

Susan sat in a seat three rows up from Levi. She was overjoyed at her good luck. Levi had become so much more than a friend and now he was working at the same place she was. *Wasn't God good,* she thought.

Levi knew that although they may not be assigned to the same area, their friendship would grow. This was the girl he wanted in his life forever. God would grant them the patience to allow this love to grow.

Someday they both would be sitting on their little park bench back home, and they would reminisce about this as they grew old together.

The Park Bench Trilogy

Martha & Joe

Chapter 1

"Happy Birthday, Mom!" The twins yelled in unison as they lit the candles on the cake they had brought to the park. Martha was surrounded by family and friends, and everyone was there to celebrate her sixtieth birthday.

"Thank you everyone. I'm overwhelmed that you all showed up to celebrate this old lady! What a surprise. Who wants to remember their sixtieth birthday?!" Laughing as she looked at everyone.

Tara and Kara had planned this party and were glad that everyone had not brought gifts. They knew their mother would throw a fit if that had happened. Tara and Kara were the only children of Martha and Bob Bounds. They were now in college and Martha lived in a small frame home about three blocks from the local park. Their father, Bob, was in heaven and they tried to make sure their mom was busy.

Sitting on the park bench and eating the delicious red velvet cake, Martha's favorite. She couldn't take it home, heaven's she'd gained ten pounds since Bob's death. She guessed it was from all the food people brought. Visions of the past entered, and she remembered the time she and Bob had met at the park. They had gone to the same high school but never dated. He was sitting with a math book from his college class, and she had come to reread, "Wuthering Heights" by Emily Bronte, one of her favorite authors.

As she remembered it, Bob had stared at his book the entire time, until she had gotten up and walked over.

"Are you going to say hello, or not?" Martha said to Bob as he finally looked up from his book. "I haven't seen you in a few years. Do you like your college classes?"

"Why Martha Johns, I haven't seen you in such a long time

either. Honestly, I wasn't sure it was you." Laughing as he stood, and they shook hands.

"Oh, come on Bob, surely a hug is in order." Grabbing him she gave him a big bear hug. Embarrassing him to death. Bob added, "Nice to see you."

Realizing she came on a little strong, she backed off, "It was so good to see you. Maybe I'll see you on campus sometime." Martha turned and walked to the bus that was pulling up. She wasn't sure it was the right one, but she was so upset with herself she got on anyway.

That's the way she had always been, just plow right on into any situation. Never giving a thought to the circumstances or what the other person might feel.

Martha's daughter, Tara, interrupted her thoughts. "Okay, Mom. What are you doing over here by yourself? You should be enjoying yourself." Pulling her mother up from the bench she made her go over to the crowd and answer a few questions.

Martha hated this, but she smiled.

"Mom, what are your plans for this new year you have begun?"

"Well, Kara, I think I'll continue working or volunteering at the shelter two days a week and going to church."

"Nothing new?" Tara asked.

"I thought I would join one of those dating sites. I get tired of cooking my own dinner. Maybe I could find someone to pay for dinner!" Laughing and smiling, she could never do that.

Kara and Tara chimed in together, "That's great."

Tara continued, "A little laughter will go a long way. You need to go to one of the comedy clubs in the area. You'd like the laughter."

Everyone began to leave, and Martha begged the girls to take the rest of the cake, so she wasn't tempted to eat it all.

"Let us walk you home, Mom, please." The twins kept saying.

"No, I'm going to sit right here and read my book. It's still early and I'll be home before it gets dark. I know my way around."

Waving good-bye the girls took off and Martha sat down to read. Most of the people had left the park, but it was still early afternoon, and the weather was perfect.

As she opened her book, Martha took a trip back to the last time they been in the park.

"Martha," Bob had called to her. "Put your book down and come here, please."

Setting her book on the bench she had walked over to the tree he was looking at closely.

"What is this?" he asked.

"It looks like some kind of fungus, Bob. Let me take a picture and you can look up what it is while I finish my chapter." Martha was used to Bob finding something unusual in nature. He was very observant.

Sitting back on the bench together, Martha read her book and Bob searched the internet for a name for this ugly fungus growing on a tree.

Suddenly, "It's a Bracket Fungus, according to the internet. Isn't that cool."

"So cool, Bob."

After the funeral she thought about this conversation over and over. Why hadn't she shown more interest? Why hadn't they walked around the park hand in hand? She missed him still.

Chapter 2

The next morning Martha headed to the homeless shelter by the church. Volunteering one day a week helped keep her busy as she helped clean up, washing, and working with the children for a while. It was good for the parents to have time to collect themselves without children around.

The shelter also had classes for the adults. If you stayed there you must attend. Most of the occupants were just down on their luck from job loss, health issues, divorce. One of the other places Martha volunteered was the Women's Center located in the same general area.

The Women's Center focused on classes for the women in interviewing, overcoming addiction, and abuse. Martha taught a class on interviewing, filling out general forms and also working on finding each person a job. Working one day a week didn't really cut it but she enjoyed her time there and would step in at other times when needed.

When Bob died, she had continued working in these two places. It kept her sane. Losing Bob had been the hardest trial in her life. She had known that God was with her, but it was a long time before she actually could put the trial in proper perspective. She questioned God. She yelled at Him. Still, He held her close. Now when she felt herself slipping, she could remember that He was always there.

Two years had come and gone, but Martha continued to keep the closet just as it was when he was alive. When Bob had left that morning, his old boots were sitting by his chair, and they were still there. Friends had tried to encourage her to make a fresh start, but she just wasn't ready.

***

Joe March sat on the other side of the park and watched the birthday party that was taking place. He noticed the twin girls and thought about his daughter and how old she would be right now, almost fifteen. He thought about his wife, daughter, and his son. That last day was hectic. Pam, his wife, was headed to the store. They had just returned from church, and everyone was so excited to start their vacation the next day.

Planning for the week at the lake, Pam had made a grocery list, so they didn't have to stop on their way to the cabin. The kids wanted to go with her as she went to buy all the goodies for the week. They had only been gone thirty minutes when the police came to his door.

They say time heals all wounds, but not for Joe. That fatal day had taken its toll on him. His hair had grayed almost overnight. He quit going to church services. He became a recluse only going out for business.

Watching the group of well-wishers, Joe was tempted to go over and wish the lady Happy Birthday. He had seen her at the park on numerous occasions, but it never seemed the right time to speak. Walking closer to the party he saw that she was turning sixty. He was thinking she looked good for sixty, he thought she was late forties. As he got closer, he saw the party winding down, so he walked on by the group smiling to the birthday girl and then walked on home.

Joe had work in the morning. He was the owner of a small company that helped remodel people's homes. Most of the work was done by the much younger guys, but Joe always met with the owner of the home first. They worked together on the project, so it was done just as the owner had hoped.

His first stop for work the next day was at the other end of his block. A lady had called and asked him to come over and discuss a remodel of the kitchen, bathroom, and master. He said he'd be there at eleven on Monday.

As Joe walked up the steps to his first appointment, he had seen the house many times when he drove down the street. Ringing the doorbell, he could hear someone inside walking to the door. As the door opened, Joe was surprised to find the lady from the park standing in front of him.

"Good morning," Joe said. "I'm Joe March from March Designs and Remodeling."

"Hey, Joe. Please come in and look around. As I said on the phone, I want to update the kitchen, bath, and master. I think the master won't be any trouble but the other two, ugh! They are a mess."

Sitting down at the kitchen table, Joe began, "What prompted you to decide on this project? You know everything will be a mess for at least a month unless you want to REALLY update the space. Are you ready for this?"

"I need to do something. My husband passed away two years ago, I feel like I'm standing still, so remodeling is first on the agenda. Maybe I won't think about where he stood or drank his coffee if I change the space up some."

Joe was instantly on guard. He knew how she felt.

He continued, "What thoughts do you have on your kitchen?" They sat and talked about the kitchen for a good while, then they looked at the bathroom and bedroom."

"I like your ideas, Joe. Could you work up an estimate and then give me a call? Hopefully it won't be too long until you could get started."

"If I get started about the first of November, I should be finished by the second week of December. Would that work for you?"

"Yes, my girls and I can go out for Thanksgiving." It would take her mind off of a Thanksgiving without Bob. "As long as it's finished for Christmas.

Chapter 3

November roared in like a lion. Martha's walks in the park were not as frequent since the ice and snow kept falling, but true to his word, Joe started on November 1ˢᵗ.

"I'm sorry this is such a hassle, Martha, but you'll get what you want!" Joe wasn't always on the job, but he would pop in and make sure his workers were doing their job. He was a good boss.

"I expected it. I've set the coffee maker up in the living area. Would you like a cup?" True to her nature Martha was always a great hostess.

Joe sat down on the couch and replied, "That would be wonderful. I'll have to get going shortly, I have another job site to check on."

"It would be great to get out. I think I'd like a job like yours except for the heavy stuff. I'm too old for that."

"You're never too old for anything! Would you like to ride along with me? I'll bring you home after my rounds. You don't have to watch over these guys, they are the best."

"Not today, I'd like to stick around at least for a while. I'm expecting a call from my daughters."

"So, you have two daughters. That's nice."

"Do you have any kids, Joe?"

Joe wasn't one to discuss family, so he pretended he hadn't heard. "Well, I suppose I need to get going. Have a good time with your girls. I'll be back later this evening at quitting time to check on everything."

Martha wondered why he didn't answer, but she didn't really want to pry. "Thanks, Joe."

Martha would have enjoyed the ride around his construction

work, but she didn't know Joe and she'd keep their friendship just that, friendship. She knew her girls wouldn't be here. They both lived too far away to come for an afternoon. If, and that's a big if, they came it would always be on the weekend.

Calling a friend, Martha thought someone might come over, they could play cards, drink coffee and gossip, but her friend was busy that afternoon. Continuing to call others she found Sue was available to come over for an hour or two.

Talking to herself, Martha wondered, "Does everyone have trouble getting friends to come over?" It was a little disheartening when you have five good friends, and none could come. She knew they had children at home, or their husbands weren't retired, but it was lonely when you had nothing to do. Maybe she should join a gym.

As she was sitting in a chair lamenting on her misfortune, the phone rang.

"Ms. Martha?"

It sounded like one of the residents at the homeless shelter. She didn't understand how they had gotten her phone number. "Yes. Who am I speaking to?"

"Ms. Martha, it's Calvin. The lady at the desk dialed your number for me. My momma was taken to the hospital. Could you come over here and get me, Ms. Martha?"

Calvin was about ten and he and his mother had been at the Women's Center for several weeks. She played cards with him while his mother was in drug counseling. "Well, Calvin, I don't know about getting you, but I can come over. Give me about thirty minutes. I'll have to walk."

"I'll be waitin' Ms. Martha."

Calling Sue, she told her something had come up and they'd have to reschedule, then she put on her snow boots and heavy coat and began the four-block trip to the building near the church that held the homeless.

The wind was biting. She should have put a scarf around her face to keep it covered, but she hadn't so she pulled the collar of her coat up over her nose and plodded along. Martha was halfway there when a truck with March Designs & Remodeling pulled up beside her.

"Need a ride." Joe said as he rolled down his window.

"That would be wonderful. I didn't realize how cold and windy it was outside."

"Where are you headed that is so important you would leave home!" Smiling at her red face, as she rubbed it to warm it up.

"The homeless shelter down from the church. One of my people was taken to the hospital and her ten-year-old son wants me to come get him. He doesn't understand that DPS will take him to a foster home. I want to lessen the blow so I'm going to hug on him for a while."

Kind and considerate. Nice lady, Joe thought. "Maybe they will let you take him home for a day or two until his mom recovers."

"I think it was an overdose, so she'll go to rehab first. Sad really. The kids get left out in the cold."

It took three minutes and they pulled into the driveway to the homeless shelter. Martha turned to thank Joe and saw he was getting out also.

"You don't have to come in with me. I volunteer here and know everyone."

"No problem. I'd like to meet this young man."

As they walked up, Calvin came running and threw himself into Martha's arms.

Chapter 4

"Whoa buddy! You're going to knock Martha down. You must be Calvin. My name is Joe, and I'm so glad to meet you." Sticking out his hand to shake Calvin's.

Calvin stared at Joe, then turned to Martha and began to beg to go home with her. "Please Ms. Martha, please take me to your house. I don't want to go with CPS. Foster homes are horrible. Please, please." Calvin was crying and pulling on Martha's arm.

Joe spoke up. "Let's go inside and talk this out, Calvin. All right?"

"CPS is here, and the papers are about to be signed. Please help Ms. Martha."

Martha hadn't been able to get a word in edgewise, so she hugged Calvin, "We will see what can be decided."

Joe took the lead as they walked into the office. The lady from CPS was young, and Joe thought he might know her. "Is that you Joann?"

The lady turned around and smiled. "Why Joe what are you doing here? I didn't know you volunteered here also."

"No, I'm here with Martha Bounds. She volunteers and Calvin is one she visits. Is there any way we can let Calvin stay with Ms. Bounds while Calvin's mother is in the hospital?"

Joann spoke to Martha, "Are you a licensed foster care worker?"

"No, ma'am but I'd do anything to get Calvin home with me."

Joann frowned, "It takes several weeks to get licensed. Joe how long did it take you to get certified?"

"Approximately two weeks. Would it be all right if Calvin were placed in my home? He could stay with Martha while I'm working and come to my place in the evening to sleep. Would that be okay with you Calvin?"

Calvin wasn't sure about this guy, but if he could stay with Martha during the day then he'd say, "Yes. I want to stay with this guy and Martha."

Joann picked up her phone and called the office explaining that Joe March would like to take Calvin for a while. The office made a few calls, and all was fine.

"Okay, Calvin. You know the rules. Pack your things and you may go with Joe."

"And Ms. Martha?"

"Yes, and with Ms. Martha?

Grabbing Joann by the waist, Calvin hugged her hard. "Thank you."

Smiling broadly, Joann replied, "You're welcome."

It had taken over an hour to settle all the decisions that were made. Everyone scrunched into Joe's truck and headed to Martha's. When they arrived, the workers were on their lunch break and since the kitchen was a total disaster Joe drove to the nearest fast food and picked up hamburgers for the three of them.

"Don't you think it would be easier for you and Calvin to stay at my house while the remodeling is going on, Martha?" Joe was concerned that it would be hectic and uncomfortable at her place.

"Maybe for a few days but once they start on the bathroom, I think we'll be okay here. I've got the refrigerator in the garage and a propane camping stove set up on my husband's old work bench. I'm sure it will work out." Martha wasn't sure at all, but as long as Calvin spent the night at Joe's all would work out, she was sure of it.

The house was in total disarray. The furniture was covered in drop cloth to keep the dust at minimum, and Martha wondered if maybe she shouldn't have gone to a friend's house while the remodel was being done. Too late. She had Calvin to worry about now.

After the hamburgers had been devoured, they loaded up and went to Joe's where Calvin proceeded to turn on the television and watch cartoons. Joe had not watched any cartoons since he had lost his children, and he was appalled at how violent they were. Getting up he walked over to Calvin, "Hey, how about we watch some good movies, okay?"

"Sure, whatever you want mister." Calvin was used to people telling him what to do, so he just complied.

Joe found some old *Gunsmoke*, and *Lassie* shows and turned them on. A little corny but *Gunsmoke* still had a little violence that Calvin would like, he was sure.

Martha walked around the living area and looked at pictures that were framed and hanging around the room. His wife had been very nice looking, and his kids looked just like him. *It's too bad he lost his entire family,* Martha thought. She had done some searching to find out more about him and saw he had lost his wife and children around the same time she had lost Bob.

"Hey, mister, this shows in black and white. What gives?" Calvin had rarely seen any television shows in B&W.

"You know Calvin," Martha began, "television was in B&W a long time ago. That's how it looked most of the time!"

"It's kinda cool." He replied.

"Well, I'm happy you like it!" Joe said as he sat next to Calvin watching an old *Gunsmoke*.

"Calvin if you don't mind, I'm going to have Joe take me home, and then you can come over in the morning. Will that be all right?"

"Sure, can we wait until the show is over? Then we can take you home, right Joe."

Chapter 5

Martha rose early the next morning. The workers would be there by eight and she wanted to be ready to go on her errands when Calvin got to the house. The workers arrived and she waited for Calvin, but he hadn't arrived by nine, so she called Joe.

"Joe, where is Calvin? I thought you'd be here by nine."

"I'm sorry, he wanted to go with me this morning to see what I do, we are on our way to your place right now."

"Oh, that's fine. Just needed to run some errands and was hoping to get going. See you in a few minutes." That was good, Calvin was comfortable.

Calvin came running inside, asking, "Ms. Martha can I go with Joe this morning? He's got a cool job!"

"If Joe wants you to then it's okay with me. I would like to play some games this afternoon and I thought we'd go visit your mother also."

Calvin thought a minute, "All right."

Martha left Calvin with Joe and headed to the grocery store then the Women's Center. She wanted to make sure it was okay to take Calvin to the hospital, but when she got to the shelter, the staff said she wasn't there. Apparently, she refused to go to rehab, and the police got involved and she was now in jail waiting for a judge.

"You've got to be kidding," Martha said. "Does she realize what this will do to Calvin?" Martha was beyond upset. She would talk with Joe later when she returned home, but right now she just needed to think.

Driving home after the store allowed her some thinking time. She would ask Joe to continue taking Calvin, and she would go to CPS and fill out the forms needed to get her certified as a caretaker.

***

In the meantime, Joe and Calvin were going from worksite to worksite. Some of the workers kept Calvin busy picking up trash and moving lumber as Joe made changes or spoke with the owners. Joe had been fairly busy for the month of November, and he prayed he would be finished by the second week in December.

Arriving back at Martha's home, he noticed she wasn't back, so he and Calvin sat in the car and talked. It seemed Calvin wanted to be adopted which took Joe by surprise.

"Calvin, what made you decide that adoption was on the table. I think you and your mom should make this decision."

"My mom is always strung out on drugs. She doesn't notice I'm around whether I'm in a shelter or on the streets. I want a home where someone will take care of me, send me to school and get on to me if I'm bad. I hate eating out of trash cans or stealing food from the store. Can you help me be adopted?"

Joe's heart sank. He would give his right arm to have his children back, and here was a little boy who would give his arm to have a family. Life was funny like that. We always wanted what we didn't have.

Joe looked up and saw Martha coming down the street. "Let's go inside, Calvin. Ms. Martha just showed up."

"Hey, guys! Why were you sitting in the truck?"

"Man talk," Joe offered. "Thought we'd come help with the groceries."

"Just take them into the garage. Most of the stuff will go in the refrigerator some in the freezer, but the cereal, bread, and donuts can be put in the cooler, so animals won't get to them."

"Donuts?" Calvin's eyes grew rounder as she questioned Ms. Martha.

"Yep, just for you young man." Martha wasn't sure how to tell Calvin his mother was in jail.

Calvin kept staring at the donuts, "Do we have to go to the hospital? I hate hospitals. Can I just stay here and play games? Joe, can you stay and play games too?"

"We can wait to on visiting the hospital, but you need to try to write your mom a short note about her being gone. Can you do that?" Martha thought maybe a note would shake up his mother.

Hanging his head, "I guess."

"Let's go in and head to the den in the very back of the house. It's quieter in there."

They all entered and headed to the back, but Martha caught Joe's arm and stopped as Calvin moved onward.

"Joe," whispering in his ear, "Calvin's mother is in jail."

"I can top that!" Joe began. "Calvin wants to be adopted!"

Bewildered, they looked at each other, "Hey you guys, come on. Let's play spades, okay?"

Chapter 6

Several weeks passed and Martha's house was getting back in order. The master bedroom was being painted, along with the kitchen and bathroom. They had put down new hardwood in the bedroom and new tile in the bathroom and kitchen.

Calvin would go with Joe in the mornings, coming to Martha's after lunch and stay until Joe got off work in the evening. Then he would go with Joe for the night. Joe often stayed and played games. Martha and Joe became comfortable and began to share what had changed their lives.

School was back in session after the snowstorm and Calvin found himself back in school. It wasn't his favorite, but as long as Joe took him and picked him up, he was happy. School came easy for him, which was surprising after all the time he had missed.

Calvin took his mother's jail time in stride, still telling Martha and Joe he wanted to be adopted. Martha and Joe had taken time to sit him down and tell him they would talk with CPS about the prospect, but they weren't sure what might happen.

One chilly evening the three were playing Chinese Checkers in front of the fireplace at Joe's house. Calvin had finished his homework and they had eaten supper early. As they played, Calvin's head nodded a few times then he laid down on the rug by the fireplace. In a few minutes he was sound asleep.

"He's a good kid, Joe. What has CPS said about his being adopted?"

"Not much really. It's usually a well-kept secret until a decision is made. I know his mother is not doing well in jail and if she gets out, she'll end up in the same place she always does, homeless."

"Joe, I'm worried. He will be devastated if he has to go back to living like that. Maybe you and I should talk to his mother."

Martha was concerned for Calvin and for Joe. Joe had grown very close to Calvin. She thought both would be lost without each other.

"I'll see if I can go during visitation tomorrow. I'm not sure I'm ready to adopt a kid, you know."

"You've never told me how your family was lost. Can you tell me what happened?"

"I can, but don't know if I want to, Martha. It was so hard. I'm sure you know that you've been through this, it's just hard to bring it up and rehash all that happened."

"Do what you think is best then."

"They died in a car crash. Several others died also. A semi-truck was out of control, ran into the back of my wife's car. Really, he ran through the car and pushed into the cab of the truck in front of my wife. The man in the truck died also. It happened in an instant."

Martha said nothing. Tears began to fall as she looked at Joe. "That was the same wreck my husband was killed also. And the semi driver died also, right?"

"Yes, it was on Highway 89, coming into town from the west. The driver had a heart
attack and that's what started the wreck." Joe was beginning to realize what she was saying.

Sitting back on the couch they both thought through the conversation they had just had, leaving little to be said.

Joe finally said, "I think it's time for Calvin and me to go. The workers will be finished tomorrow. I'll see you later in the day." Walking over to Calvin, he picked him up and carried him to the truck.

***

"Joe, why are we leaving? Put me down. I can walk." Calvin was not happy about leaving.

"It's time to go Calvin. You were sound asleep. No need to stay."

"You know if you and Ms. Martha got married you could adopt me!"

Was this what Calvin had been thinking? Joe thought. He

needed to set Calvin straight.

"First, young man, I don't have to marry anyone to adopt you. Second, Ms. Martha and I aren't that kind of friends."

Pouting, Calvin said, "Well you could be!"

They drove quietly home, not speaking, and when they arrived Calvin went straight to his room.

***

Martha sat on the couch just thinking about her life and how it had rushed forward since Bob had died. She would love him forever. He shaped her life and gave her so much. She was so glad that God had brought him to her and that they had loved each other completely.

Now it was time to move on. She had cleaned out the closet, the kitchen, and the bathroom. Bob wouldn't recognize the house, and she wouldn't recognize him in it. Maybe it was time, as the girls kept saying, to join a dating site, OR maybe not.

Chapter 7

The remodeled house was a boost to Martha's morale. She spent several days finding new curtains, bedspread, pillows, and even bought new pots and pans even though she didn't need them. She continued her volunteer work and now that she was certified to work for foster care, she stayed very busy. Martha loved having Calvin after school several days a week and he was thriving. Unfortunately, his mother wasn't doing as good and would soon be let out of jail.

Walking to the park Martha still continued to enjoy reading at her favorite park bench. She went at least three times a week. It was so fun to watch the people, and especially the children. One day her girls would marry and have children and she was excited for that journey to begin. As she came to her bench, she found Joe and Calvin sitting and watching her as she walked up.

"Well, I didn't expect to see you all here. Did you just come from school? It's a little early to be out of school, isn't it?"

Joe spoke up, "Yes, it is. We have been to the jail to see Calvin's mom. Calvin why don't you explain why?"

"I wanted her to sign papers for me to be adopted. She cried and cried. Told me she was sorry that she was such a horrible mother. I told her she wasn't horrible. I still love her. I just want a family that isn't always running from stuff."

Martha was impressed with Calvin. Very grown up for such a young boy. "What was her response?"

Calvin smiled, "She said she understood. Then she said okay, tell me what to do and I'll sign papers so you can be adopted. Isn't that great!"

Joe looked at Martha with concern. "Calvin, why don't you take your new skateboard to that area (pointing to where he should go).

Maybe those kids can give you some lessons."

Calvin jumped up, grabbed his skateboard, and took off.

"Why do you look so concerned, Joe? Isn't this great?" Martha was a little confused.

"Hold onto your hat, Martha, cause Calvin wants us to get married so he can live with us."

Martha's eyes were wide with unbelief. "Yes, you heard me correctly."

"Where would he get an idea like that? We've never given him that impression, at least I don't think so."

"Remember when we talked, and he fell asleep in front of the fire. Well, as I was carrying him out to the truck, he mentioned it. I just laughed it off, but he was downright serious!" Joe shrugged his shoulders and continued to look puzzled.

Martha began to laugh, "This is hard to believe, Joe. I mean I think you're a great guy, but I'm at least ten years older than you. Why would he think we would marry? We've never even been on a date."

"Kids say the funniest things. I guess if we sit him down and tell him to quit wishing maybe things will be better. How about taking him to dinner and talking to him together?"

"When?" Martha had plans for two nights that week. The dating app she joined had kept her hopping, but most of the men were not what she was looking for.

"Why not tonight? Get it over with."

"Well, Joe, I joined this dating app, like my girls suggested and I have a coffee date tonight. How about tomorrow?"

Joe started laughing uncontrollably. "Why would your girls think you needed an app to find a date? You are a beautiful woman, and if I hadn't been around your party, I would have guessed you to be in your late forties. How have the dates been?"

Martha looked offended at first, then she began to laugh. "It's been awful. The guys are tottering older me who think they are the gift all ladies would like. And they aren't. I've left early from every date. You're probably right. I should get out of this."

"You meet men all the time. Workers, volunteers, church, the

park. Cancel your date, we'll have a real date with food tonight."
Joe hadn't known she was dating.

"All right. Where do you want to meet?" Martha felt silly after they had discussed the dating app problems.

"Nope, Calvin and I will pick you up at six tonight and we'll go to the best steakhouse in town."

Joe whistled for Calvin, and he came running. "We need to get home. The three of us are going out to eat tonight."

Calvin jumped up and down. "Yippee!"

Chapter 8

Joe and Martha took Calvin to dinner and explained that if he wanted to be adopted, he'd need to look further than the two of them. He didn't understand, but by the end of dinner he was resigned to looking and going to other's homes.

"You know Calvin, you need a family with other children. Brothers and sisters have a way of making life so much better." Martha wanted him to think further than two older people. Although she figured Joe was about fifty.

"That's right. What would you do with this old man?"

"Exactly what I'm doing now. Just loving you." Tears came to Calvin's eyes.

Martha almost started crying. "Let's forget that for now. Let's eat and have a good time. I love being with all of you. Things have started looking up since I met both of you!"

Joe liked having Calvin around, but he also liked having Martha around. They met several times at the park and walked the two miles around for exercise and then sat at their favorite bench. He didn't know why it was his favorite, but it was.

As Joe was dropping Martha off later that evening, he asked, "Would you like to go bowling this weekend? Calvin seems to love it, so I figured you'd like to come."

"Are you sure you want me to tag along? I'm not much of a sports person anymore." Martha thought it would be fun, but she didn't want to butt in on their time together.

Calvin spoke up, "No I want you to come."

"Then of course I will be happy to beat you all in bowling!" Laughing as she continued. "I played on a league until the girls went off to college so watch out."

Martha opened the truck door, "Thanks guys. I enjoyed the

evening." Closing the door, she walked to her porch and turned around and waved. She was beginning to like Joe more than she realized and looked forward to seeing him each time he came around.

That night as Joe hopped into bed, he thought how much Martha had added to his life. He liked her more than she even realized, but Calvin needed all his attention right now. Joe must make sure Calvin was settled before he got himself into a full relationship.

The next morning Joe called Calvin's case worker and set up a meeting about Calvin being adopted. It would be a slow process, but Calvin could stay with him until he met his forever family if the court agreed.

Joann was waiting for Calvin and Joe when they arrived at her office. "Good morning. How is everyone this morning?"

Calvin flew right in and began talking, "I want to be adopted, and my mom said okay. Can you find me a family?"

"Slow down Calvin. There are a few steps we must go through first. I need to secure your mother's signature on some documents that she gives up her parental rights. That might take a few weeks. We have to petition the court and then the next process is to find you a family. What about you Joe?"

"We've talked, but I think a young boy needs a family, maybe a brother or a sister. He needs to learn family things. All I do is work." Joe would love to adopt Calvin, but . . ..

"Well, let me get all the paperwork started and I'll give you a call in about a week or two. Will that work, Calvin?"

"Yes, ma'am."

***

Martha's daughters were coming in for Christmas break. Tara and Kara had plans to go skiing the day after Christmas with a group from the college. Martha was excited to see the girls, and Christmas was always special. When Bob was still living, they all would go skiing after Christmas, but now it was just the girls and their friends.

Martha had invited Joe and Calvin for dinner and gifts on Christmas Day and of course they had said yes. Kara was excited to meet Joe and especially Calvin.

"Mom, how long have you and Joe been seeing each other?" Kara tried to be discreet but that was never her strong suit.

"We haven't been seeing each other, Kara. Joe remodeled the house and Calvin is one of the homeless children where I volunteer. It's a long story, but I believe Calvin will be adopted shortly by a couple who have adopted a little boy already. That would give Calvin a brother too!"

Tara chimed in, "I thought Calvin was living with Joe."

"Joe is his foster parent at the moment." Martha wasn't about to tell the girls how Calvin wanted her and Joe to marry and then adopt him.

"Well from what I've heard from you, I think this Joe is someone interested in you and by the look on your face you're interested in him. Mom, it's time to move on!"

"Listen girls, do not bring this up around Joe or Calvin. False hope is not good and besides I'm at least eight years older than Joe." Martha was trying to change the subject.

Kara began, "Tsk, Tsk, mom age doesn't matter once you're grown up. You should be ashamed of yourself for being so judgmental. Joe might really be interested in you and yet you put him down because of your age. Whatever happened to let God take care of this?"

"That's right," Tara threw into the conversation. "When I was dating Jimmy, you always told me to not worry. If he was 'the one' then God would give me a sign."

Martha threw up her hands. "Okay, I give up. Just let me handle it my way!"

Chapter 9

Everyone had a wonderful time during the holidays. The girls came home from their skiing trip just in time to head back to school. Martha was glad when life got back to normal. She loved her children but even at twenty they were a handful.

The weather had been cool but dry and the park had been full of walkers, children, and chess players. When the sun was blazing the weather seemed almost spring like, but it wasn't time for January. Martha hadn't seen Joe in a week. He had been in court with Calvin, and they visited when they could.

The trees were bare, and it allowed the wind and the sun access to everyone below. Walking to her favorite bench she sat down and let the sun beat on her to get warm. Closing her eyes, she thought of the times she had seen Joe sitting on this bench and now she wondered when she first realized she felt something for him. Her mind kept saying, I'm sixty he's around fifty-two. I'm too old.

Opening her eyes, she found Joe's blue eyes staring at her face. "Hello, Martha."

"Hi, Joe. What are you doing here?" Martha was taken aback by the expression on his face.

Joe just smiled. "How long are we going to keep doing this, Martha?"

"Doing what? I was just enjoying the sunlight on my face. It tends to warm my frozen body on days like this. Where are you headed? I thought you'd be at work. Is Calvin still at school?"

Joe quietly said, "Shh, no more chatter. Martha, I think I've fallen in love with you. I know it came out of the blue, but whenever I'm with you I feel at peace. I don't know how you feel, but I'd like to know."

Martha took a deep breath, "Joe you know I'm a lot older than you. I wasn't looking for anyone. I thought we were just good friends. We were helping Calvin. I don't know what to say."

Joe shook his head, smiling, "I know this is unexpected. Let's do this, I'll meet you halfway. I want us, just you and me to go on some adventures. Dinner, the carnival, church, the library, I don't care where, but I think inside you know I'm right. We are made for each other. In six months if you don't see it, I'll go my own way."

"See what, Joe?" Martha couldn't take her eyes off his.

"See that you love me, want to marry me, understand."

"You think that will take six months?" Martha could tell him that now, but she was afraid.

"No, do you?"

***

Six months later Tara and Kara walked Martha down the aisle. Calvin looked smart in his new suit and was the best man for Joe. He and his adopted family came to the Central Baptist Church to celebrate the marriage of Joe March and Martha Bounds.

The vows were traditional, the couple was traditional and when the preacher finished, he traditionally said, "You may kiss the bride." Joe waited not one minute more.

"For what God has joined together, let man not separate."

Made in the USA
Middletown, DE
04 September 2022